Home for
Christmas

THE PATIO
CLUB™

WRITTEN AND ILLUSTRATED BY
CARYN MOTTILLA

Home for
Christmas

Home for Christmas
The Patio Club®
Published by Open Window Publishing
Castle Rock, CO

Publisher's Cataloging-in-Publication data

Names: Mottilla, Caryn, author.
Title: Home for Christmas / by Caryn Mottilla.
Description: First trade paperback original edition. | Castle Rock [Colorado] : Open Window Publishing, 2019. | Series: The Patio Club.
Identifiers: ISBN 978-0-9997471-1-7
Subjects: LCSH: Old age—Fiction. | Christmas stories. | Short stories.
BISAC: FICTION / General.
Classification: LCC PS374.O43 | DDC 813–dc22

Cover design by Caryn Mottilla

QUANTITY PURCHASES: Schools, companies, professional groups, clubs, and other organizations may qualify for special terms when ordering quantities of this title. For information, email ThePatioClub@gmail.com.

OPEN WINDOW
PUBLISHING

The Patio Club® is dedicated to the men and women in assisted living communities, memory and Hospice care who have listened to the adventures of The Patio Club™. They expressed their hope for these stories to be published and shared with others across the country.

An Introduction to The Patio Club

The Patio Club was originally formed by two sets of sisters—Elaine and Adele from New Jersey, and Betty and Mildred from Kentucky. The women were young when they met in the 1940s. The years passed by, and later in life, the four adventurous women made a pact that after they died they would meet up and visit retirement and assisted living communities. After they passed away, they came to Happy Visions Retirement Home and liked it so much they decided to stay.

The women call themselves "The Patio Club," because they sit outside on the patio of Happy Visions. Each day, Elaine, Adele,

Betty and Mildred are surrounded by colorful sparkles, and they meet a steady stream of interesting visitors and residents who pass through Happy Visions on their way to unknown destinations.

One amazing thing is that the Patio Club can look to the sky and watch a video of each person's life. This precious gift lets the Patio Club understand the unique story that each person carries with them.

Home for Christmas

IT WAS A FEW WEEKS BEFORE CHRISTMAS AND soft, white snow blanketed the evergreen trees on the patio behind Happy Visions Retirement Home. The snow looked like puffs of cotton. The Patio Club dusted the snow off of the metal lawn chairs that they sat on each day. The purple cloud-filled sky showed the remains of the super-moon that lit last evening's sky and made the moon look like a giant snowball.

The women sat on the cold, metal patio chairs talking about Christmas. It was just a few weeks away. Many

of the residents of Happy Visions no longer shopped for Christmas gifts. They were lucky to celebrate this special holiday without the burden of shopping.

Each day as dusk descended, the women of the Patio Club watched as the warm lights of Happy Visions Retirement Home streamed through the windows of the residents' rooms. Many of the residents went to bed early. However, Elaine, Adele, Betty and Mildred noticed there was one particular room where the lights were on till late at night, and the window to the room was open.

The women of the Patio Club were very curious about the light and the open window. "Who could be up this late?" Betty asked. With sparkles trailing behind them like stars in the late-night sky, the women quietly walked over to the window where the light was streaming onto the frozen patio.

The women of the Patio Club stood silently in the dark and looked in the window with great curiosity. They were surprised when they saw a young woman with golden blond

hair sitting at a small dining table holding a Christmas snow globe. She did not know that the Patio Club was watching her as she lifted the snow globe and shook it, then sat it back down on the small table.

The window to the young woman's room was cracked open, and, as she shook the snow globe, the Patio Club heard her say, "Please come home for Christmas."

Well, the Patio Club was fascinated by this! They looked at each other with excitement. Adele whispered, "Who is she and what is she doing here?" When Elaine, Adele, Betty and Mildred looked back into the room, the young woman with the blond hair was gone and sitting in her place at the same small dining table, shaking the snow globe, was an older woman. She had hair the color of snow and she wore the same flowered flannel nightgown that the young woman had worn just moments earlier.

"What the heck is going on?" asked Betty. "Did you see what I just saw?" They were stunned by what they had just seen. First, it had been a young woman sitting at the

table in a flowered flannel nightgown shaking a Christmas snow globe. When they had looked back, the young woman was gone and in her place was a much older woman with snow-white hair shaking the same snow globe and saying, "Please come home for Christmas."

Then the older woman placed the snow globe next to a lamp on the nightstand beside her bed. A bright red quilt trimmed in gold covered her full-sized bed. She pulled back the quilt, climbed into bed and turned off her bedside lamp.

Well, as you can imagine, the women of the Patio Club were in shock! "Who is she?" Elaine whispered as golden sparkles danced in the air.

That's when Adele told them that she had often seen this woman sitting in the corner of the dining room each day. Even when other residents were at her table in the dining room, she seldom spoke. She had arrived a few months ago, with little fanfare and no visitors since then.

Each evening just after dusk, the lights in the woman's room would come on and cast a stream of welcoming golden light onto the patio. As the days passed by leading up to Christmas, the Patio Club watched with delight as the woman turned on the small lamp by her bed and picked up the snow globe. She walked slowly in her flowered flannel nightgown to the small dining table near the open window.

Through the slightly open window, the four women would watch the young woman with the golden blond hair appear. She would lift the snow globe and shake it saying, "Please come home for Christmas." Minutes later, the young woman would change into the older woman who the other residents saw each day. Then the older woman would slowly walk to her bed with the soft, red quilt with gold trim, climb into bed and turn off the light. The warm light in this woman's room was always the last one to go out at night. The window to her room would stay cracked open—even if it was snowing outside.

Elaine, Adele, Betty and Mildred loved being in the Patio Club. It seemed that each day, and certainly each week, they would see the most amazing things for people who were in the last years of their lives. The older residents were fearless in imagining what was possible. Each night, the Patio Club cheered with amazement when they watched both the young and old woman shake the snow globe and repeat the same phrase, *like it was magic*, "Please come home for Christmas."

It seemed that Elaine, Adele, Betty and Mildred were the only ones witnessing the nightly snow globe ritual. Elaine said that it was like being in a Christmas story. They had no idea what the wish meant or even if it would come true.

The four women began to use a few simple strategies to find out the story behind the snow globe and the wish that the woman made each night to "Please come home for Christmas."

First, the Patio club *guessed* at what the wish might

mean. Elaine was the first to speak. "I always loved dogs. Maybe the woman lost a dog when she was a child and wished each Christmas for the dog to return home."

"Good guess," said Adele. "Maybe the woman had lost her boyfriend or husband in war and each Christmas she hoped he would come back. That would be my guess."

"That is possible," said Mildred. "The woman may have lost her son or daughter at Christmas and waited each year for her child to return. That would be my Christmas wish."

Betty was not much of a romantic. However, even Betty ventured a guess. "I believe the woman's Christmas wish is for someone who had died to return." Then Betty continued, "Mildred and I were in our thirties when we lost our sister at Christmas in 1959."

Betty continued to recall the loss of her sister during the holidays. "My children remembered that I was not home that Christmas. Santa brought them big dolls that stood

by their beds *like sentries guarding them* until I returned. My guess is that the woman is secretly wishing for her sister to come home for Christmas."

It was Christmas Eve, and Walter the retirement home dog walked onto the patio. Trailing behind him were a few red and green sparkles. Walter looked and saw Elaine, Adele, Betty and Mildred as they stood outside of the older woman's window waiting for her nightly ritual. The wind was blowing and snow flurries sprinkled the air like the ones that sparkled in the snow globe. Walter stood with the Patio Club, sniffing the frosty air. His tail wagged like a flag, signaling that he sensed someone new was in the area, but no one was around.

The four women and the dog heard the older woman through the slightly opened window. Her chair creaked as she sat at the small dining table. Suddenly they heard the old woman *winding a button on the snow globe* and it began to play a Christmas song!

Elaine, Adele, Betty and Mildred looked at each other

as the snow globe's song began to play, "I'll be home for Christmas." The excitement at hearing the song quickly moved through the Patio Club and even Walter the dog! It felt like a "zing" that tickled them and filled them with the kind of joy that children feel at Christmas.

When the song stopped, the group watched with wonder as the young woman with golden blond hair transformed into the old woman. As the snow in the globe settled, the Patio Club watched the old woman smile as she repeated her nightly wish, "Please come home for Christmas." Something, however, was different tonight. The smile that crossed her face gave the impression that she was confident her wish would come true.

The Patio Club "shushed" each other, hoping to quiet their excitement! Even Walter gave a soft bark and his wagging tail spread sparkles and snow flurries behind him now.

As the others walked away, Betty stood in silence at the open window. She watched the moonlight shining

through the open window, reflecting off of the snow globe. Suddenly, Betty realized that maybe what was happening was in some way meant to bring peace to her and Mildred.

Betty's and Mildred's sister Helen had died in 1959, and Helen's son had died tragically a few years before. That Christmas, Betty and Mildred could not understand why their sister Helen would pass away at Christmas. They had heard of people who could postpone dying for months so they did not miss birthdays or holidays.

Betty turned from the window, and brilliant white sparkles followed behind her as she walked over to where Elaine, Adele and Mildred stood with Walter. Then Betty asked Mildred if she ever wondered why their sister Helen had left at Christmas. Mildred thought for a moment and then a smile came across her face. She quietly chuckled and said, "Maybe Helen's son would visit her after he died and ask her to 'Please come home for Christmas.'"

Finally, the Patio Club decided to use their special gift of being able to look to the sky to watch the video of the

woman's life, the woman who shook the snow globe each night. They watched the video as it played against the ink-colored winter sky.

In the video, they saw a handsome man standing with his beautiful, young bride at the entrance to a church. The bride had long, golden blond hair. The video continued and showed the couple riding bicycles through a neighborhood and waving to their neighbors. The woman's hair was shorter now with streaks of gray. The years flew by like pictures in a deck of cards. Finally, the Patio Club watched as the older woman stood in front of the same church where she was married. She was much older now, her hair was white and her handsome husband was gone. People came to the church that day to celebrate her husband's life.

The video continued and showed the woman's first Christmas without her husband, and that's when the snow globe appeared. It was Christmas Eve, and the woman looked sad as she sat alone at the dining room table. She shook the globe back then saying, "Please come home for Christmas."

Suddenly, a bright light filled the room that first Christmas through a slightly opened window. As snow fell outside and the woman's Christmas tree colored lights lit up the living room, she saw her husband standing before her. He looked like an angel! He smiled and said to her, "I promised you that if you made a wish that I would come back each year for Christmas, honey."

The women of the Patio Club were crying tears of joy. They went back to the window and watched as the older woman walked slowly to her bed. A stream of twinkling red and green sparkles trailed behind her now. She placed the snow globe on her nightstand. Then she slowly turned back the bright red quilt trimmed in gold, climbed into bed and turned off the light. She left the window opened slightly as she did each night.

Something was *very* different tonight. There was a soft light glowing in the room that seemed to come from nowhere. The woman with hair the color of snow had a smile on her face, and it seemed as though someone had climbed into bed beside her.

Elaine, Adele, Betty and Mildred and even Walter the dog stood watching all of this. They were amazed by what they had witnessed. As they looked on the ground below the woman's window, they saw a trail of a man's footprints in the snow. They knew that the woman's wish for her husband to come home for Christmas had come true.

As the women of the Patio Club looked one last time to the video in the sky, they saw the older woman snuggled in the red quilt-covered bed. She was young once again with golden blond hair, a handsome, young man dressed in green flannel pajamas lay beside her, holding her while she slept.

For those who are BRAVE enough to make a wish at Christmas, may all of your wishes come true *especially the ones you carry in your heart.*

Merry Christmas from the Patio Club!

The End.

The Patio Club's Story

IN NOVEMBER OF 2016, I began writing fictional stories for retirement and assisted living communities. This occurred because of a simple request from an older gentleman in his 80s who asked if I could write a story about people "their age." Writing and telling stories has always come easily to me. I happily said , "yes." I was excited at the challenge and have written a story each month since then. They are about a fictional retirement/ assisted living community named *Happy Visions*. Each month I read to retirement and assisted living communities. The joy of doing this is overwhelming.

In July of 2017, I was reading to a group of older women as they sat outside *on the patio* in the shade. The women's ages reached up to 95. When I left the patio that day, I decided at that moment to write a story for them called "The Patio Club." The series began with that story.

The stories I write come effortlessly to me. It is as if I am divinely inspired. As I began writing the first story in the Patio Club series, I was so surprised as I watched the story come to life. It is the story of two sets of sisters, Elaine and Adele from New Jersey, and Mildred and Betty from Kentucky. They made a pact that when they died they would meet up and visit retirement and assisted living communities.

Imagine my surprise—because in real life Elaine and Adele (sisters) were my aunts from New Jersey, and Betty (my mother) and Mildred (my aunt) were sisters from Kentucky! My Aunt Mildred was the last one to join The Patio Club. She passed away earlier in 2017. The Patio Club™ stories now touch people from around the country and hopefully someday from around the world.

My dream is that The Patio Club™ series will be read to the people in assisted living, memory and Hospice care communities. As I read each month to these special people, I realized that it is often difficult to visit loved ones who are in the assisted living population. What I have found is that reading a story seems to transform everyone from the reader to the listener. I have seen people with all kinds of health challenges perk up when listening to the joyful adventures of The Patio Club™. They are in the present moment as they listen and during that time there is nothing wrong with them.

My wish is that people will take the adventure of reading a story (about 12 to 15 minutes) from The Patio Club Series to a loved one. It will transform the visit from one where it may be difficult to find something to talk about, to one where both the reader and listener are moved beyond words.

With gratitude and love,

- Caryn

Acknowledgments

THE PATIO CLUB is dedicated to my aunts Elaine, Adele, Mildred, and my mother Betty. Although the characters in the Patio Club are fictional, they are based on these important women who impacted my life.

Special thanks to my sons Carson and Cooper, as well as, family and friends who have listened to these stories. They have enthusiastically cheered for me to follow my dream to write and illustrate stories that bring joy and adventure to the lives of others.

Finally, I am grateful to God for the gifts He has given me to serve the people in assisted living, memory and Hospice care.

About the Author

CARYN BEGAN WRITING children's stories for her children in the 1990s. In 2016, as she read children's stories to assisted living communities, residents asked her to write a story "for people their age." That was how the adventure of writing for the adult and assisted population began.

Since that time, Caryn has written a monthly series called The Patio Club™. It takes place at a retirement home/assisted living community named Happy Visions. The Patio Club™ are the first stories published by Caryn for that age group. The stories have captured the attention of people of all ages across the country.

The Patio Club™ stories are a bridge between the reader and the listener. Family and friends that visit assisted living, memory and Hospice care communities may struggle for something to talk about. Reading a story like The Patio Club™ to these special residents takes them on an adventure without them ever having to leave the room. It creates an opening for some interesting conversations!

Caryn lives in Colorado. She has two grown sons, Carson and Cooper